TINY TED

Peter Bowman

HUTCHINSON

London Auckland Sydney Johannesburg

Inspired by Bonningate

First published in 1994

1 3 5 7 9 10 8 6 4 2

Peter Bowman has asserted his right under
the Copyright, Designs and Patents Act, 1988
to be identified as the author of this work

First published in the United Kingdom in 1994 by
Hutchinson Children's Books
Random House, 20 Vauxhall Bridge Road, London SW1V 2SA

Random House Australia (Pty) Limited
20 Alfred Street, Milsons Point, Sydney,
New South Wales 2061, Australia

Random House New Zealand Limited
18 Poland Road, Glenfield
Auckland 10, New Zealand

Random House South Africa (Pty) Limited
PO Box 337, Bergvlei, South Africa

Random House UK Limited Reg. No. 954009

A CIP catalogue record for this book
is available from the British Library

ISBN 0 09 176177 8
Printed in China

From the case on the wall came a big sigh.

'I'm fed up with
being on the shelf,'
said Tiny Ted.

'No one ever
talks to me…'

'…and just look at the
dust and cobwebs!'

'I wonder
what the
world is like
down there...'

'Atishoo!'

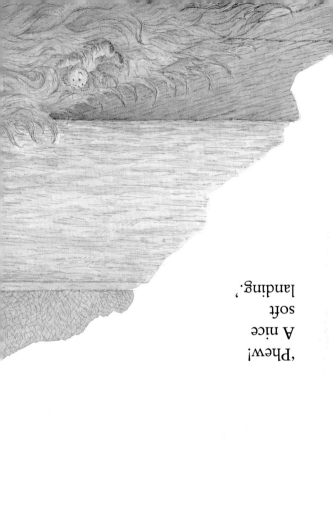

'Phew!
A nice
soft
landing.'

'Oh no!
It's not a mat.
It's a cat!'

'Phew, that was close.
I think I'll hide
behind these logs.'

'Oh, what lovely colours!'

'Hey! It's that cat again.'

"Help!"

'It's chasing me!'

'Goodness! It's not very safe down here.'

'I think I'll just
hide in this box
until the coast
is clear.'

'Oh, no! It's somebody's house.'

BOING!

'Where am I now? Eeeek, MONSTERS!'

'I've had enough.
Will someone please
take me home?'

'Just a little bit higher...'

'…Whoops!
Not high
enough.'

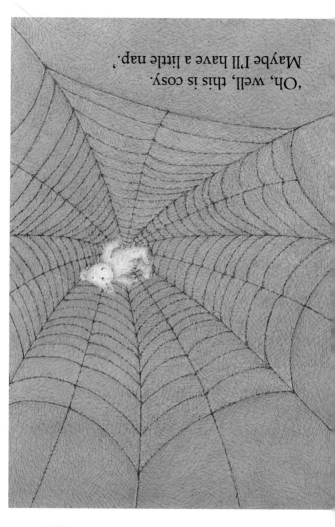

'Oh, well, this is cosy.
Maybe I'll have a little nap.'

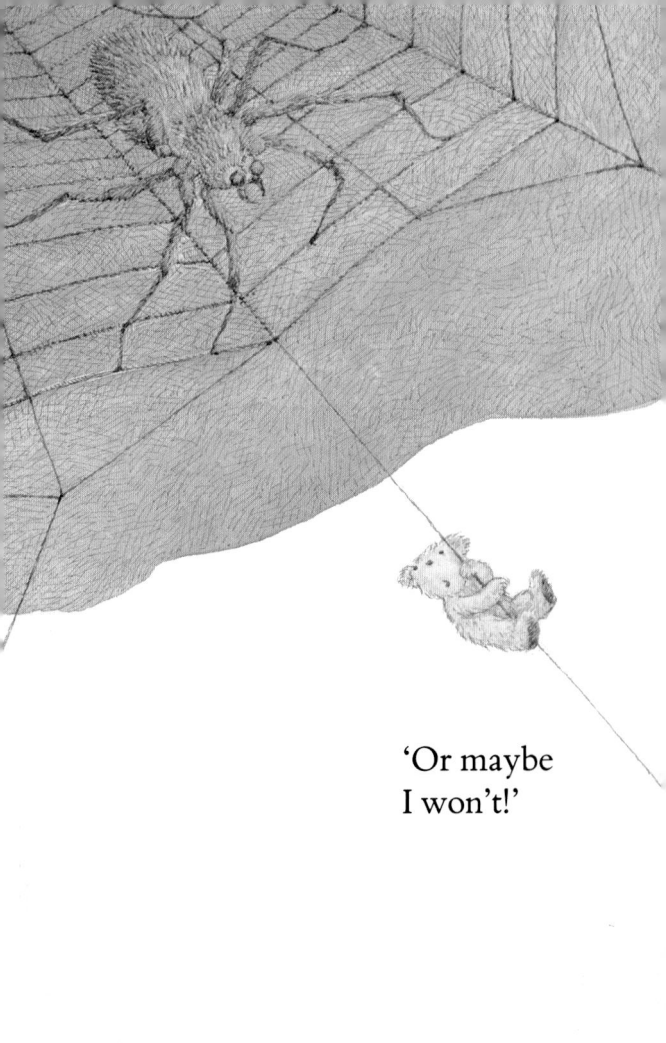

'Or maybe
I won't!'

'Hello, I'm Tiny Ted.
I'd love to dance.'

'But I've gone all dizzy.'

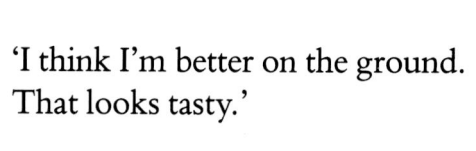

'I think I'm better on the ground.
That looks tasty.'

'Ouch! My paws,'

'Whoops. Pardon me.
It's just that I'm lost
and alone, and very,
very small.'

'Oh, you are kind,'
said Tiny Ted.
'Safe at last!'
And he was.